Your child's love of reading starts here, with HarperAlley's **I Can Read Comics!**

HARPER *alley*

**I Can Read Comics** introduces children to the world of graphic novel storytelling and encourages visual literacy in emerging readers. Comics inspire reader engagement unlike any other format. They ask readers to infer and answer questions, like:

1. What do I read first? Image or text?
2. Why is this word balloon shaped this way, and that word balloon shaped that way?
3. Why is a character making that facial expression? Are they happy, angry, excited, sad?

From the comics your child reads with you to the first comic they read on their own, there are **I Can Read Comics** for every stage of reading:

| LEVEL 1 | LEVEL 2 | LEVEL 3 |
| --- | --- | --- |
| Simple stories for shared reading. | Engaging stories for children reading on their own. | Complex stories for independent readers. |

The magic of graphic novel storytelling lies between the gutters. Unlock the magic with…

# I Can Read Comics!

Visit **ICanRead.com** for information on enriching your child's reading experience.

# I Can Read Comics Cartooning Basics

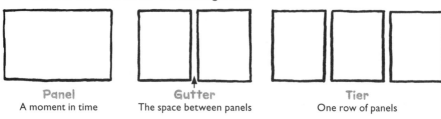

| Panel | Gutter | Tier |
|---|---|---|
| A moment in time | The space between panels | One row of panels |

## Word Balloons
When someone talks, thinks, whispers, or screams, their words go in here:

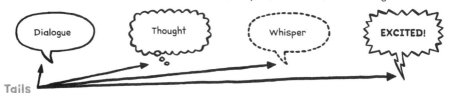

Dialogue  Thought  Whisper  EXCITED!

## Tails
Point to whoever is talking / thinking / whispering / screaming / etc.

## A quick how-to-read comics guide:

In a **panel**, read the text on the **left** first.

Then, read the text on the **right**.

On a page, **start here**, in the **top left** corner!

After that, read the panel immediately to the **right**.

When you're done up there, come down here and read **this** panel next!

ME NEXT! ME NEXT!

You're almost there...

YOU MADE IT! You just read a comic page!

YAY!

## Remember to...
Read the text along with the image, paying close attention to the character's acting, the action, and/or the scene. Every little detail matters!

## No dialogue? No problem!
If there is no dialogue within a panel, take the time to read the image. Visual cues are just as important as text, so don't forget about them!

Pete the Cat: Making New Friends
Text copyright © 2021 by Kimberly and James Dean
Illustrations copyright © 2021 by James Dean
Pete the Cat is a registered trademark of Pete the Cat, LLC.
All rights reserved. Printed in the United States of America.
No part of this book may be used or reproduced in any manner whatsoever without written permission except in the case of brief quotations embodied in critical articles and reviews. For information address HarperCollins Children's Books, a division of HarperCollins Publishers, 195 Broadway, New York, NY 10007.
www.icanread.com

Library of Congress Control Number: 2021936853
ISBN 978-0-06-297414-3 (trade bdg.) — ISBN 978-0-06-297413-6 (pbk.)

Book design by Chrisila Maida
21 22 23 24 25  LSCC  10 9 8 7 6 5 4 3 2 1  ❖  First Edition

# I Can Read! Comics

LEVEL 1

# Pete the Cat

## Making New Friends

by Kimberly
& James Dean

HARPER alley

An Imprint of HarperCollinsPublishers

# Meet Secret Agent Meow.

Also known as Pete.
Pete the Cat.

Gizmo watch,
what new case
do we have today?

When there is a mystery...
Agent Meow is **always** on the case!

# A new case falls into Agent Meow's lap.

Agent Meow asked his gizmo watch for a clue.

But Grumpy loves to skateboard.

16

Agent Meow asked his gizmo watch for another clue.

But Callie loves ballet.

Agent Meow asked his gizmo watch
for another clue!

But Emma loves to paint.

That's not tapping!

Right!
But you and Callie both love to **dance**.

24

A little while later...

Wow!

Tap!
Tap!
Tap!

Do you want to swap?

When you are lonely and don't know what to do, try to find someone who enjoys the same things as you!

And so
Secret Agent Meow
solves another case...